Richard Scarry's STORYTIME

Random House New York

 Published in the United States by Random House, Inc., New York, and simultaneously in Canada by Random House of Canada Limited, Toronto. ISBN: 0-394-83338-4. *Library of Congress Catalog Card Number:* 76-11630. Manufactured in the United States of America.

A SUMMER PICNIC

It was a bright, sunny summer day.
There was not a cloud in the sky.

Miss Honey and her boyfriend, Bruno,
decided to take all the children on a picnic.

They drove past a lake where
some fishermen were fishing.
Oh, oh! They seem to have
caught something!

While they were setting out the picnic, Rudolf Strudel, the famous airplane pilot, dropped by.

"Miss Honey!" he said. "A big thunderstorm is coming. You and the children must take shelter immediately!"

Everyone had been too busy putting out food
to notice the black storm clouds gathering.

“Hurry!” Rudolf warned. “The rain will start any minute.”

C-r-a-a-a-a-c-c-k-k-k!
The lightning flashed! The thunder roared!
But everyone was safely inside the school-bus.

No one got even the tiniest bit wet.
Not even Farmer Fox's tractor.
It was the best rainy-day picnic ever.

LIFE GUARD
LIFE GUARD

A RESCUE BY AIR

Al, the lifeguard, sat on his stand, watching the swimmers. It was his job to rescue any swimmers in trouble.

Suddenly Al heard someone shouting, "HELP!"

He jumped down from his stand and rushed into the huge waves.

It was Mathilda.

The wind had carried her too far from shore.
She couldn't swim back.

But Mathilda was too big for Al to save.
Now who would rescue *him*?

What good luck!
Just in time
the Coast Guard
helicopter came
to the rescue.
It lifted Al
and Mathilda
out of the sea.

The helicopter flew them safely back to the beach, where Huckle unhooked them.

Mathilda promised Al that she would be more careful the next time she went swimming on a windy day.

SPEEDBOAT SPIKE

Speedboat Spike liked to take his little boy, Swifty, out for a ride in his speedboat.

Oh, my! Didn't Spike think he was smart!

Once he rammed a sailboat.

Another time, he bumped into a barge . . .

. . . and knocked a lady's wash overboard.

Spike just wouldn't slow down . . .

. . . and he wouldn't stop bumping into things.

But that was before Officer Barnacle caught him . . . and made him stop!

Officer Barnacle ordered Speedboat Spike to keep his speedboat in a wading pool . . . UP ON LAND!

Now Spike can go as fast as he likes, without bumping into anyone.

POLICE

But who is that
in the tiny little
speedboat?
Why, it's his little boy,
Swifty!

Oh dear! We are going
to need another wading pool.

Go get him, Officer Barnacle!

THE PIE RATS

Not a soul dared to go sailing.
Do you know why?
There was a wicked band of pirates about,
and they would steal anything they could get
their hands on!

But Uncle Willy wasn't afraid.
"They won't bother me," he said.

He dropped his anchor
near a deserted island.

Aunty Pastry had baked him
a pie for his lunch.

"I think I will have a nap
before I eat my pie,"
said Uncle Willy to himself.

Uncle Willy went to sleep.
B-z-z-z-z-z.

What is THAT I see climbing
on board?
A PIRATE! And another!
And another?
PIRATES, UNCLE WILLY!

But Uncle Willy couldn't do a thing.
There were just too many pirates.

First, they put Uncle Willy on the deserted island. Then they started to eat his pie. "M-m-m-m-m! DEE-licious!" they all said.

Uncle Willy was furious. But then he had an idea. He gathered some long beach grass, which he wove into a kind of cloth.

Then he tied some sea shells onto some branches and made a ferocious-looking mouth.

He tied the grass cloth onto the mouth,
then attached some sea-shell eyes.
By the time he tied on a spiky palm leaf,
he had made a ferocious MONSTER!

Uncle Willy got inside. He was now "Uncle Willy,
the FEROCIOUS MONSTER."
Look out, you pirates!

The Ferocious Monster swam out to the boat.
The pirates were terrified.
They all ran into the cabin to hide.
The Ferocious Monster closed the door
behind them—and locked it.
He had captured the wicked pirates!

Then the Monster sailed back home.

Uncle Willy landed and took off his monster suit.
Everyone said, "Thank goodness it was only you!"
Sergeant Murphy took the pirates away to be punished.
Well . . . Uncle Willy had made the seas safe to sail on again.

Hurray for Uncle Willy—
THE FEROCIOUS MONSTER!!!

SERGEANT MURPHY'S DAY

Sergeant Murphy was busy putting parking tickets on cars when, suddenly . . .

. . . who should come running out of the market but Bananas Gorilla. He had stolen a bunch of bananas and was trying to escape.

Huckle and Lowly Worm were watching.

Look, Murphy! He is stealing your motorcycle, too!

Sergeant Murphy was furious. Huckle said, "You may borrow my tricycle to chase after him."

Away they went, chasing after that naughty thief . . .

. . . through the crowded streets.

Don't YOU ever ride your tricycle in the street!

They crossed a drawbridge just as it
was opening to let a boat go through.

Well done, Sergeant Murphy!

Bananas stopped suddenly . . .

. . . and went into a restaurant.

Murphy said to Louie, who was the owner,
"I am looking for a thief!"

Then Louie said,
"Sit down and relax, Murphy.

Together, they searched the whole restaurant, but they couldn't find Bananas anywhere.

I will bring you and your friends something delicious to eat."

Louie brought them a bowl of banana soup. Lowly said, "I'll bet Bananas Gorilla would like to be here right now."

"Huckle, we mustn't forget to wash our hands before eating," said Sergeant Murphy. Lowly went along too.

When they came back, they discovered that their table had gone.

Indeed it was slowly creeping away when . . .

. . . it slipped on a banana skin!
And guess who was hiding underneath.

Sergeant Murphy, we are proud of you! Bananas must learn that it is naughty to steal things.